THE SCIENCE ZONE

The Funny Zone

Read Jokes. Write Jokes.

Jokes, Riddles, Tongue Twisters & "Daffynitions"

By Gary Chmielewski

Illustrated by Jim Caputo

A Note to Parents and Caregivers:

As the old saying goes, "Laughter is the best medicine." It's true for reading as well. Kids naturally love humor, so why not look to their interests to get them motivated to read? The Funny Zone series features books that include jokes, riddles, word plays, and tongue twisters—all of which are sure to delight your young reader.

We invite you to share this book with your child, taking turns to read aloud to one another, practicing timing, emphasis, and expression. You and your child can deliver the jokes in a natural voice, or have fun creating character voices and exaggerating funny words. Be sure to pause often to make sure your child understands the jokes. Talk about what you are reading and use this opportunity to explore new vocabulary words and ideas. Reading aloud can help your child build confidence in reading.

Along with being fun and motivating, humorous text involves higher order thinking skills that support comprehension. Jokes, riddles, and word plays require us to explore the creative use of language, develop word and sound recognition, and expand vocabulary.

At the end of the book there are activities to help your child develop writing skills. These activities tap your child's creativity by exploring numerous types of humor. Children who write materials based on the activities are encouraged to send them to Norwood House Press for publication on our website or in future books. Please see page 24 for details.

Above all, the most important part of the reading experience is to have fun and enjoy it!

Sincerely,

Shannon Cannon

Shannon Cannon
Literacy Consultant

NorwoodHouse Press

P.O. Box 316598 • Chicago, Illinois 60631
For information regarding Norwood House Press, please visit our website at: www.norwoodhousepress.com or call 866-565-2900.

Designer: Design Lab
Project Management: Editorial Directions

Library of Congress Cataloging-in-Publication Data:
Chmielewski, Gary, 1946–
  The science zone : jokes, riddles, tongue twisters & daffynitions / by
Gary Chmielewski ; illustrated by Jim Caputo.
     p. cm. — (The funny zone)
  Summary: "Book contains 100 science-themed jokes, tongue twisters and "Daffynitions". Backmatter includes creative writing information and exercises. After completing the exercises, the reader is encouraged to write their own jokes and submit them for future Funny Zone titles. Full-color illustrations throughout"—Provided by publisher.
  ISBN-13: 978-1-59953-183-0 (library edition : alk. paper)
  ISBN-10: 1-59953-183-6 (library edition : alk. paper) 1.
Science—Juvenile humor. I. Caputo, Jim. II. Title.
PN6231.S4C46 2008
818'.5402—dc22   2007045532

Manufactured in the United States of America

OUT IN SPACE

How do you get an astronaut's baby to fall asleep?
Rocket!

Why did the earthling fall in love with the alien?
She was 'out of this world'!

3

Alien: "I was born on the planet Neptune."
Scientist: "That's amazing. Which part?"
Alien: "All of me!"

ASTRONOMER
Night watchman with a college education.

What's a light year?
The same as a regular year only with fewer calories!

How did the astronaut serve dinner in outer space?
On flying saucers!

One astronomer asks another if he has ever heard of the planet Saturn. The second astronomer replies, "I'm not sure, but it has a familiar ring!"

What part of the keyboard do astronauts like best?
The space bar!

Why is an astronaut like a football player?
They both want touchdowns!

Star light, star bright.
First star I see tonight.
I wish I may, I wish I might.
Darn – it's just a satellite!

Where do astronauts leave their spacecraft?
At parking meteors!

After eating his first meal on the moon, the astronaut reported, "The freeze-dried food was good, but the place lacked atmosphere!"

BLACK HOLES
What you get in black socks.

Why did Mickey Mouse go into outer space?
He was looking for Pluto!

PLUTO OR BUST

THE SUN & MOON

Teacher: "There will be an eclipse of the moon tonight. Perhaps your parents will let you stay up and watch it?"
Tina: "What channel is it on?"

How does the barber cut the moon's hair?
Eclipse it!

What holds the sun up in the sky?
Sunbeams!

What is the moon worth?
$1 – it has 4 quarters!

Which is more useful – the sun or the moon?
The moon, because it shines at night when you want the light, whereas the sun shines during the day when you don't need it!

What did the sun say to the earth when they were introduced?
"Pleased to heat you!"

THE EARTH

Never lend a geologist money. They consider a million years ago to be recent.

What did one cloud say to the other?
"I'm cirrus about you!"

How do hurricanes see?
With one eye!

What did the father volcano say to the mother volcano?
"Do you lava me like I lava you?"

Lisa Marie was born on December 27th, yet her birthday is always in the summer. How can this be?
She lives in the Southern Hemisphere, where the seasons are reversed from those in the Northern Hemisphere!

What is a flood?
A river that is too big for its bridges!

What did one tornado say to the other?
"Let's twist again, like we did last summer …"

How much dirt is there in a hole exactly one foot deep and one foot across?
None – a hole is empty!

What doesn't get any wetter, no matter how much rain falls on it?
Water!

How do you spell hard water with 3 letters?
I-C-E!

Kathleen: "Are you still dating that geologist?"
Shannon: "Yes. I like him despite all his faults."

LIFE SCIENCE

What did the slime say to the mold when they saw each other after a long while?
"You gruesome since I saw you last!"

Fungi Class Reunion

One microbe ran into another microbe while moving through the bloodstream.
"You don't look so hot," said the first microbe.
"I feel terrible," said the second. "I think I'm coming down with penicillin!"

In biology class the teacher was explaining that germs always work in large groups.
Emily, the class clown, piped up, "That would explain why no one has ever come down with the measle."

Why did the amoeba take two aspirins?
Its head was splitting!

What's full of holes but still holds water?
A sponge!

Even if they are starving, a native living in the Arctic will never eat a penguin's egg. Why not?
There are no penguins in the Arctic – they are native to Antarctica!

You are in a room with 3 monkeys. One has a banana, one has a stick, and one has nothing. Which primate in the room is the smartest?
You are the smartest. Remember humans are primates too.

If we breathe oxygen during the day, what do we breathe at night?
Night-rogen!

PHYSICAL SCIENCE

Why did the atom cross the road?
It was time for him to split!

What did the boy battery say to the girl battery?
"I get a big charge out of you!"

Maria: "They say that Isaac Newton discovered the law of gravity when an apple fell on his head."
Darrell: "Was it a laptop or a desktop model?"

What can be measured but has no length, width, or thickness?
The temperature!

What do physicists enjoy doing the most at ballgames?
The 'wave'!

What is the center of gravity?
The letter 'v'!

What weighs more: a pound of lead or a pound of feathers?

They weigh the same – a pound is a pound!

What's the formula for water?
H_2O.

What's the formula for an ice cube?
H_2O-cubed!

Teacher: "How fast does light travel?"
Tannia: "I don't know, but it gets here too early in the morning!"

Two atoms bump into each other. One says, "I think I lost an electron." The other asks, "Are you sure?" to which the first replies, "I'm positive!"

What did Benjamin Franklin say when he discovered electricity?
Nothing. He was in shock.

How much do used batteries cost?
Nothing, they are free of charge!

Where does bad light end up?
In a prism!

Lupita: "Lisa, name a unit of electrical power."
Lisa: "What?"
Lupita: "Right, the watt is absolutely correct."

Have you heard the one about the chemist who was reading a book about helium and just couldn't put it down?"

A chemist walked into a pharmacy and asked, "Do you have any acetylsalicylic acid?"
"Do you mean aspirin?" asked the pharmacist.
"That's it! I can never remember that word," explained the chemist.

What's the most important thing to learn in chemistry?
Never lick the spoon!

Old chemists never die – they just fail to react!

What do you do with dead elements?
Barium!

Why do chemists like nitrates?
They're better than day rates!

Why are chemists great for solving problems?
They all have solutions!

COMPUTER SCIENCE

If at first you don't succeed ...
... call it version 1.0.

Why was the computer so tired when it got home from the office?
It had a hard drive!

What did one computer keyboard say to the other keyboard?
"Sorry, you're not my type!"

Why do spiders do so well in computer classes?
They love the web!

Why was Emily's father kicking the computer?
He was trying to boot it up!

CLASS IN SESSION

Did you hear about the young boy who plans to be an astronaut?
His teacher says he's just taking up space!

Why do hippies study the stars?
Because they are so 'far out'!

Why did the 25-watt bulb flunk out of school?
He wasn't very bright!

School Librarian: "Tannia, have you read any mysteries lately?"
Tannia: "I'm reading one now."
School Librarian: "What's it called?"
Tannia: "My science book!"

James was really excited when he came home from school. His mother asked him for the good news and he said, "I got a hundred in school today! In two subjects!" James's mother was overjoyed. "My goodness, how did you do that?"
James replied, "I got a fifty in math and a fifty in science!"

IN THE LAB

Why did the astronomer hit himself on the head in the afternoon?

He wanted to see stars during the day!

EXPERIMENT
What scientists did over 100 years ago and you are still doing in school!

How do mad scientists freshen their breath?
With experi-mints

Who was the smartest inventor?
Thomas Edison. He invented the phonograph so people would stay up all night and use his light bulbs.

Why do scientists look at things twice?
Because they re-search everything!

How did the scientist invent bug spray?
She started from scratch!

How do you turn a regular scientist into a mad scientist?
Step on her toes!

If an experiment works, something has gone wrong!

WRITING JOKES CAN BE AS MUCH FUN AS READING THEM!

A pun is a joke that uses words in funny ways. One way to make a pun is to take a word that sounds a lot like another word (or words). Next you switch the words, or make a *play on words*, to create the joke. It is important to remember that puns are very short and you get to the punch line quickly. You can often take a pun and turn it into a riddle. Here is an example from page 18:

What do you do with dead elements?
Barium!

This is funny because *barium* is the name of a chemical element, and it sounds a lot like the words *bury 'em*, which is what you do with something that is dead.

Go back and re-read the jokes in this book. Which of them are puns? Which ones do you think are funny? Try to figure out why you think they are funny.

YOU TRY IT!

Here is a joke-writing exercise you can do by yourself or with some friends who enjoy science. Find a copy of the Periodic Table of the Elements. Read through the names of the elements and try to think of words or short phrases that sound very similar to the names of some of the elements. Write down a few of the elements and the words or phrases that sound the same. Then try to come up with jokes that use the plays on words you've come up with. Try the jokes out on some people. Just make sure that they know something about science, because if they don't, they won't understand your jokes! Keep the jokes that get big laughs, and keep working on the ones that don't. Then, the next time your science teacher is in a grumpy mood, tell a good element joke—it might just get you a laugh and some extra credit!

SEND US YOUR JOKES!

Pick out the best pun that you created and send it to us at Norwood House Press. We will publish it on our website — organized according to grade level, the state you live in, and your first name.

Selected jokes might also appear in a future special edition book, *Kids Write in the Funny Zone*. If your joke is included in the book, you and your school will receive a free copy.

Here's how to send the jokes to Norwood House Press:

1) Go to www.norwoodhousepress.com.
2) Click on the **Enter the Funny Zone** tab.
3) Select and print the joke submission form.
4) Fill out the form, include your joke, and send to:
   The Funny Zone
   Norwood House Press
   PO Box 316598
   Chicago, IL 60631

Here's how to see your joke posted on the website:

1) Go to www.norwoodhousepress.com.
2) Click on the **Enter the Funny Zone** tab.
3) Select **Kids Write in the Funny Zone** tab.
4) Locate your grade level, then state, then first name.
   If it's not there yet check back again.